T·H·E
CANTERBURY
·TALES·

For Emma and David   S.H.

For Ann   R.C.

GEOFFREY CHAUCER
c.1342-1400

Text copyright © 1988 by Selina Hastings
Illustrations copyright © 1988 by Reg Cartwright
All rights reserved, including the right to reproduce
this book or portions thereof in any form.
First published in Great Britain by
Walker Books Ltd., London
Published in the United States by
Henry Holt and Company, Inc., 115 West 18th Street,
New York, New York 10011.

Library of Congress Cataloging-in-Publication Data is available.
Library of Congress Catalog Card Number: 88-45163
ISBN: 0-8050-0904-3

First American Edition

Printed and bound in Italy by L.E.G.O., Vicenza

1 3 5 7 9 10 8 6 4 2

ISBN 0-8050-0904-3

T·H·E
CANTERBURY
·TALES·

BY

GEOFFREY CHAUCER

A SELECTION

RETOLD BY
SELINA HASTINGS

ILLUSTRATED BY
REG CARTWRIGHT

HENRY HOLT AND COMPANY · NEW YORK

CONTENTS

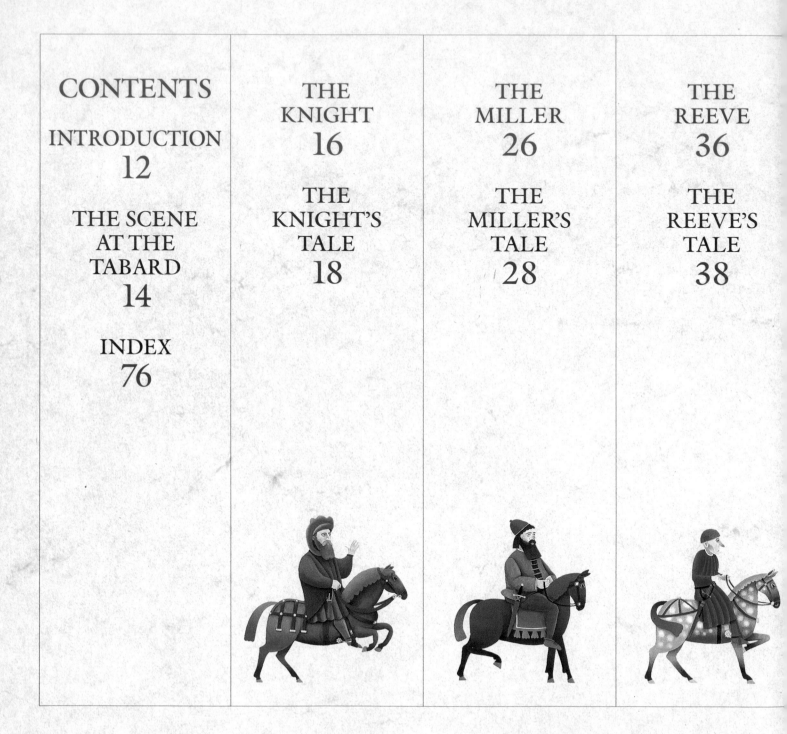

INTRODUCTION

Geoffrey Chaucer, often called "the father of English poetry," was born in about the year 1342, and probably died in 1400. He was the first of a long line to be buried in what is now known as Poets' Corner in Westminster Abbey. His father had connections in the wine trade, and Chaucer himself made a successful career in the medieval equivalent of the civil service. As a boy he was employed as page to John of Gaunt, Duke of Lancaster; he fought in France during the Hundred Years' War; and he became an important member of the household of Edward III, frequently travelling abroad on the King's business. During the reign of Edward's successor, Richard II, Chaucer left London and the court to live in Kent, where he was appointed Justice of the Peace and Knight of the Shire.

In 1386 he retired from office for a period of three years, and it is believed that during this time he began to write *The Canterbury Tales,* without question the greatest narrative poem of its kind in the English language.

In England and much of Europe in the Middle Ages, good Christians, either as a gesture of thanksgiving or repentance, or simply as an affirmation of faith, tried at least once in their lives to make a pilgrimage to one of the famous holy places – perhaps to the shrine of St. James of Compostella in Spain, or to that of Our Lady at Lourdes, or even as far as Jerusalem itself. In England one of the most frequented routes was that from London to the tomb of the martyr St. Thomas à Becket in the cathedral at Canterbury.

It is not known whether Chaucer himself ever made this particular pilgrimage, but as a narrative device (a company of pilgrims on the road) it is superb. The journey itself, from the Tabard Inn at Southwark in the City of London to Canterbury, would have taken several days, and Chaucer's plan was for thirty or so pilgrims each to tell four stories, two on the way there, two on the way back. His scheme was never completed. Nonetheless, we are left with twenty-four tales and an unforgettable group of characters which, both by status and temperament, provides a wide cross-section of fourteenth-century England, from the nobly born and virtuous Knight, with his story of sacrifice and chivalry, to the rascally Miller, whose chief interest lies in trickery. Both the Knight's and the Miller's Tale are included in this book, together with five other stories notable for the vigour of both characters and plot.

❧

One April evening there arrived at a tavern in Southwark a party of pilgrims preparing to go the following day to Canterbury. The innkeeper welcomed them warmly, and having provided them with wine and a good supper, addressed them thus: "Let me make a suggestion for your journey. To my mind, there's no fun to be had riding along in solemn silence. What I propose is this: that

as you go, each of you in turn shall tell a story, and he whose story gives the most pleasure shall be treated by the rest to a splendid dinner here on your return. If you like this idea, I myself will go along with you to be the judge!"

The pilgrims delightedly agreed, and when they set off early the next morning for Canterbury, the inn-keeper rode with them. As they went, he made them all draw lots to see who should be the first to tell a tale....

The Knight

was of all the pilgrims the truest gentleman.

He had fought bravely for

his King and country both at home

and abroad, and his reputation

was as great for modesty, courtesy and

a sense of honour as for

courage on the field of battle.

THE KNIGHT

THE KNIGHT'S TALE

DUKE THESEUS, that great soldier and ruler of Athens, was riding back one day from a campaign at the head of his army when, nearing the walls of his city, he passed on the highway a company of women dressed in black. They were kneeling by the side of the road, howling with grief and tearing their hair. As the Duke approached, one of the women caught at his bridle.

"Oh, Sir, have pity on us!" she cried. "We are all widows, our husbands slain in battle by King Creon of Thebes. He, cruel man, has refused us permission to bury our dead and now their bodies lie rotting on the plain to be devoured by dogs. I implore you, my noble Lord, to avenge this terrible injustice!"

Theseus was moved by the widow's words and, gently raising her to her feet, promised he would do everything in his power to punish the tyrant. Although they were nearly home, he at once ordered his men to turn round and march to Thebes. Arriving outside the city walls Theseus loudly challenged the Theban King to battle. He himself fought so fiercely that, by the end of the day, Creon was dead, his troops put to flight and the city razed to the ground.

That night the Athenian army lay encamped on the edge of the battlefield. To Theseus in his tent were brought the unconscious bodies of two young men who had been identified by their coat of arms as belonging to the Theban royal house. The Duke recognized the princes as cousins, Palamon and Arcita. He was delighted to have made such an important capture and gave orders that their wounds be dressed and that they should then be sent to Athens, there to be kept prisoners for life.

And so they were, and so they lived for several years, locked up in a great stone tower with no hope of escape.

One May, early in the morning, the Duke's sister, Emily, happened to be wandering through that part of the palace garden which was overlooked by the tower where the two Thebans were imprisoned. Emily was young and beautiful, her figure slender, her complexion as fresh as the rosebuds she was gathering. While she walked, Palamon by chance looked out of the window, a small window high in the tower and set with iron bars. He saw Emily, started, turned pale, and gave a cry as though he had been stabbed. Arcita, beside him, clutched his cousin's arm. "Palamon, what's the matter? Are you ill? Are you in pain?"

"Oh, cousin, I have been wounded, wounded to the heart, by that divine creature, that goddess, walking down there in the garden. I am madly in love with her!"

Arcita turned to look. He, too, saw Emily; he, too, staggered back, clutching his heart. "Oh, what beauty! What loveliness! I shall die if that woman cannot be my wife!"

Hearing these words, Palamon looked grim. "Oh, you traitor! Are we not blood brothers? I trusted you with my heart's secret and now you are trying to steal my love from me. *I* loved her first! You, as my brother, are bound in honour to help me win my love!"

"No, indeed, cousin, it is you who are false! I was the first to love her as man loves woman: you took her for a goddess. My love is the real one; it is *you* who should be helping *me*. But why quarrel? We both know that all is fair in love and war. And what can either of us do about it here in prison? Good luck to both of us, I say, and let us bear it as best we can!"

It so happened that shortly after this the Duke's oldest friend, Perotheus, came to visit him. Perotheus had known Arcita well in Thebes and so he asked as a personal favour that the young man should be released from prison. To this Theseus consented, but he made it a condition that Arcita, on pain of death, should never set foot on Athenian land again.

So Arcita returned to Thebes – not, as one might expect, rejoicing at his liberty but full of lamentations at the cruelty of his fate. "Alas, how miserable I am," he wailed, "banished for ever from the sight of my beloved! How happy is Palamon in prison! What am I saying? Not in prison but in paradise! He is free to see Emily every day, while I, poor wretch, may never set eyes on her again!"

Palamon, meanwhile, alone in his tower, found it little comfort that he was able to look on Emily, but never reach her. The thought of Arcita at liberty made him howl like a dog with jealousy and rage. "How unjust that Arcita should be free! He will go to Thebes, raise an army and return to carry off Emily to be his wife! While I, poor Palamon, remain shut up until the day of my death within the walls of this gaol!"

In Thebes Arcita was pining away for love, unable to eat, unable to sleep, pale as a ghost, thin as an arrow. Soon he had faded away to a mere shadow, hardly recognizable even to his closest friends. And in this state he continued for two years, until it suddenly came to him in a dream that he should defy Theseus' ban and go at once to Athens. "I will see Emily once more, if I die in the attempt!" he cried, leaping from his bed. Seizing a mirror, he looked closely at his reflection: as he thought, he had grown so thin that, if disguised, he could live in Athens without anyone knowing who he was.

And this is just what happened. Dressed as a poor labourer he managed to get himself taken on as a man-of-all-work at Theseus' court where he could see Emily every day. Here he proved himself so able that within two years he had risen to the position of steward to the Duke himself.

Poor Palamon, now in the seventh year of his imprisonment, had finally grown desperate. By means of a well-placed bribe he procured a strong sleeping powder which he slipped into his gaoler's wine. And, while the man slept, he broke out of the tower. Quickly moving through the dark streets of the town he soon came to open country, to a wood where he thought it would be safe to lie concealed during the hours of daylight.

The next morning dawned brilliantly and Arcita, waking early, decided to ride out and gather flowers in celebration of the month of May. Without knowing it he came to the very grove where Palamon lay hidden. Here he dismounted and, wandering happily among the flowers, broke into song. Palamon, crouched behind a bush, instantly recognized Arcita's voice and, in a burst of rage, leapt out at him. "Arcita, you traitor! You are the cause of all my misery! I have no weapon with me now but hear my challenge: either fight to the death or give up your love for Emily!"

"You fool," Arcita scornfully replied. "I am free to love where I choose. But I accept your challenge and will meet you tomorrow on this spot. I will bring arms for us both to decide our fate!"

The following day Arcita returned bringing with him two suits of armour and two swords. Having helped each other arm, the cousins unsheathed their weapons and began to fight.

Now it so happened that Theseus chose that morning to go hunting. With his wife, Hippolyta, and Emily and a company of courtiers, he rode out towards the wood which was well known to be a likely place to find deer. There he came across the Theban princes

battling furiously like a couple of wild boars. Pulling out his sword Theseus reined in his horse and shouted, "Stop! He dies who moves! No more, on pain of death! Tell me who you are and what is the cause of your quarrel!"

Palamon was the first to catch his breath. "Sire," he panted, "we were both your captives. I, Palamon, have only last night escaped from prison; and this is Arcita, whom you banished from your land and who, in disguise, has been living as a servant in your household. Both of us love your sister Emily. And both of us deserve to die!"

Theseus responded angrily. "You stand condemned by your own words and die you must!" But before he could say more Hippolyta and Emily, moved by pity for the two young noblemen, intervened and begged the Duke to spare their lives. As they pleaded Theseus felt his anger subside.

"Well, well," he said at last. "You have both suffered enough in the cause of love and I am prepared to pardon you. But Emily can't marry you both so this is what I propose: that you return to Thebes and come back here twelve months from this day, each with a company of a hundred knights. You shall then meet in pitched battle. One of you must either be taken captive or be killed and to the other I will give Emily's hand."

So Palamon and Arcita returned to Thebes to raise their companies of knights and prepare for battle. Theseus gave orders for the laying-out of a great tourney-field. It was more than a mile in circumference with a magnificent arch of white marble at either end. Beside one arch was erected a temple to Venus, goddess of love, and at the other an altar to Mars, god of war.

Twelve months passed and the day came when Palamon and Arcita, each with a company of one hundred brave and noble knights, returned to Athens.

The following morning Arcita got up before dawn and made his way to the temple of Venus where he prayed to the goddess to help him. As he rose from his knees he thought he saw her statue move, which he took as a sign that she would be on his side.

Palamon, meanwhile, had gone to the temple of Mars, to whom he made a sacrifice so that the god would make him the winner. As he spoke his prayer, the fire on the altar blazed up and from the flames he heard a voice whisper, "Victory."

The two men, well pleased, returned separately to the palace to present themselves to Theseus. The Duke, sitting in state on his throne and surrounded by the whole court, received them kindly. "I have no wish," he said, "for any man this day to lose his life. And so I decree that only single combat be allowed and no weapon other than a sword be carried on the field." A cheer went up and immediately both spectators and combatants began to hurry along the narrow streets of the city to the arena. Here Theseus, Hippolyta and Emily took their seats in the royal box.

Palamon, carrying a crimson banner, took his stand with his knights under the Martian Gate at the very moment that Arcita, under a white banner, entered with his troop by the gate of Venus. The heralds proclaimed the rules, the trumpets sounded and the battle began. The two armies galloped at full speed onto the field. Swords flashed; hooves pounded; some men fell and were carried quickly away; others, tumbled from the saddle, battled on foot.

No one fought more bravely than Palamon and Arcita. Sweating and bleeding, their armour dented with blows, they at last came face to face. While they stood for a moment, each with his sword raised, one of Arcita's knights came up behind Palamon and threw him to the ground, declaring him captive. Theseus rose to his feet. "The battle is over!" he cried. "Stop the fight! Arcita is the victor. To Arcita I give my sister Emily as wife!"

The crowd roared. The trumpets blared. Arcita, his eyes blazing, leapt up into the saddle and galloped triumphantly round the ring. But all at once his horse stumbled and he was thrown to the ground. Four men came running forward and, lifting him onto a litter, carried him back to the palace. It was soon clear that nothing could save him. Knowing that he was near death, Arcita asked that Emily and Palamon should be brought to his bedside.

"Emily," he whispered, "I have loved you more than life itself and now, alas! I must leave both you and life. It is for you that I have made an enemy of my cousin Palamon. But now that I am about to die, I commend him to you. You will not find a better man than Palamon upon the earth." And with his last breath he took Emily's hand in his and pressed it to his lips.

Theseus gave orders for a royal funeral. Palamon and Emily wept as though their hearts would break as they watched the flames devour the mortal remains of the prince they both had loved.

Many months of mourning followed Arcita's death but then there came a day when Theseus summoned Palamon and Emily before him. "Out of the double sorrow for you, Palamon, and my sister Emily, let us make one perfect joy. You, Emily, must take Palamon to be your husband and your lord. Come, Palamon, take your lady by the hand."

And so Emily and Palamon at last were wed and from that time forward neither of them knew one moment of unhappiness.

The Miller

was a big man, all brawn and bone

and as strong as an ox.

He was a bit of a buffoon,

had a fund of dirty stories to tell

in the tavern, and was a

master-thief when it came to stealing

the grain brought to him to grind.

THE MILLER

THE MILLER'S TALE

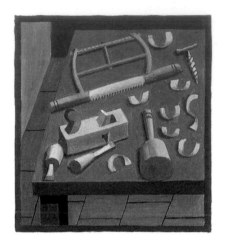

IN ENGLAND, in medieval times, there lived in Oxford a prosperous carpenter who had taken into his house a poor student as a lodger. Nicholas was this student's name and although he was good at his books, his real interest lay in the study of astrology. He could, if the stars were right, forecast the weather and tell those who consulted him if their luck was in or out. He was well known for this – but what few people knew about was his skill at wooing girls. He was a great success with women, being a good-looking lad, always clean and well turned out; he had a sweet singing voice, too, and often accompanied himself on the harp.

Now the old carpenter, whose name was John, had recently married for the second time, his new wife a young girl of only eighteen. She was pretty and high-spirited and knew very well how to dress and make herself attractive. Most men would have fancied her – and her old husband, knowing this, kept a close watch, jealous of any man who so much as looked at his adored Alison.

One day, when the carpenter was out, Nicholas began to flirt with Alison. At first she was skittish, giving a little shriek when he tiptoed up behind her and put his hands round her waist. "Don't do that, Nicholas!" she cried. "No, I won't kiss you! Take your hands away!" But Nicholas was so persuasive and spoke so sweetly to her that she began to relent, and in no time at all was promising that she would be his. But they must be careful.

"My husband is very jealous," said Alison. "It would be the end of me if he caught us together!"

"Oh, don't worry about that," said Nicholas. "A clever chap like myself can outwit a simple old carpenter any day of the week. Just leave it to me!"

The next day was Sunday and Alison, as usual, went to church dressed, as usual, in her most becoming cap and shawl. Now one of the parish clerks, whose job it was to assist at divine service, had been making eyes at pretty Alison for some time. His name was Absalon, a vain, good-looking boy who, for a churchman, spent far too much time on his appearance. His blond hair was always neatly curled, his complexion pink and freshly scrubbed, his jacket dashingly styled and sewn with ribbons and flounces. He knew all the latest dances, had a small but charming singing voice and was able to play both the guitar and the violin.

This Absalon imagined himself in love with Alison, ogling her in church whenever the parson's back was turned and squeezing her fingers when he took round the collection plate. That Sunday, after the service was over, Absalon made up his mind to try to win her. He waited until night had fallen, then, taking his guitar, went off to the carpenter's house. Here he stood under the bedroom window and began to sing a love song he had composed himself. This of course woke old John, lying asleep beside his wife. "Do you hear that noise, Alison? It's that fool, Absalon, caterwauling outside the window!"

"Yes, yes, John, I hear him," said Alison soothingly. "Take no notice; he'll soon give up and go away."

But Absalon had no intention of giving up. The more resolutely Alison ignored him, the more love-lorn he became, following her about like a little dog as she went on her errands around the town, serenading her underneath her window at night. But Alison cared not a jot for Absalon. Her heart belonged to Nicholas.

At last the two lovers had their chance: John the carpenter went off to Osney for the day, leaving Nicholas and Alison free to lay their plans. What they decided on was this: Nicholas, taking some food with him, was to go up to his room and stay there silently. When John returned and wondered where his lodger was, Alison was to say that she didn't know, she hadn't seen or heard of him all day.

And so it turned out. Nicholas lay dozing on his bed, John came home, and by the following morning the carpenter indeed began to worry. "What can have happened to Nicholas?" he asked his wife. "He's very quiet. Perhaps he's ill, or worse still, dead! I'd better go upstairs and have a look."

So up he went and hammered on the door and, getting no reply, bent down to peer through the keyhole. There he saw Nicholas lying unmoving on his bed, mouth agape, eyes wide and staring at the ceiling. "Lord bless us!" exclaimed the carpenter. "The boy's in a trance! This is something to do with that astrology he's always messing about with!" And putting his shoulder to the door, he burst into the room. Still Nicholas didn't move. John, by now thoroughly alarmed, shook him by the shoulder and shouted loudly in his ear. "Hi! Nicholas! Wake up, boy! Come back to life! What's happened to you?" He shook him again and this time Nicholas responded, blinking and muttering to himself, "Will it really happen? Is this really the end of the world?"

"What *are* you talking about?" said John. "What do you mean — the end of the world?"

Slowly Nicholas stood up. He yawned, he stretched, he scratched his head. Then he looked wonderingly around him. "Bring me some ale," he said, "and I will tell you what I know."

The carpenter hurried off to get a jug of his strongest ale, returning within minutes and shutting the door firmly behind him.

"Now, John, my friend," Nicholas began, "you must swear on your honour never to repeat a single syllable of what I am about to say, except to your wife, to Alison. If you break your word, I give you this warning — God's vengeance will fall on you!"

"Say no more, lad. I'll not tell a soul!"

Taking a deep breath and looking the carpenter solemnly in the eye, Nicholas then began to spin his tale. "By means of my astrological calculations, I have worked out that on Monday next, round about midnight, rain will start to fall and in such torrents that within

30

an hour the whole world will be flooded. It will be twice as bad as the Flood in the Bible – and nobody will be left alive! All humankind will be destroyed!"

The carpenter went white and clutched Nicholas by the arm. "Is this true? Are we all to drown? Is there nothing that can save us?"

"Well," said Nicholas, "there is a way." He paused. "You, me and Alison can all be saved if you do exactly what I say. Just as in the Bible God saved Noah and his family, so it has been revealed to me how the three of us may be saved. Now, listen carefully. You must find three wooden barrels, big enough for a man to sit in. With some strong rope tie these barrels to the rafters, having placed in each an axe and enough food to last one day. We will take refuge in the barrels and when the rains stop we can cut ourselves down and float free on the waters. After that, we'll have the whole world to ourselves!"

At this the carpenter, old John, turned at once to go, eager to carry out his instructions. But Nicholas held him back. "One more thing," he said. "Once in our barrels we must not make a sound, but hold our tongues and pray for our salvation."

So the Monday following, John trotted off to find three barrels and hoist them to the ceiling, as he'd been told. This done, he went to find Alison and tell her of Nicholas's clever plan to save the three of them from drowning. Now Alison knew very well that this was all a trick but she pretended to her husband to be faint with fear, promising to obey him in everything if only he would save her life.

That night, as soon as it was dark, the three of them climbed up by ladder into the barrels hanging from the roof. There they crouched, not speaking a word, waiting for the rain to fall.

As Nicholas had foreseen it wasn't long before the carpenter, tired out by his exertions, fell asleep, his snores reverberating through the whole house. Nicholas and Alison, quiet as mice, crept down their ladders and hand in hand disappeared into Alison's chamber.

Meanwhile Absalon, the lovesick clerk, not having seen the carpenter about his work that day, thought it safe to assume that John was away from home. "I'll risk it," said Absalon to himself. "I'll stay awake tonight and just before dawn I'll go to Alison and ask her for a kiss. With her husband away she'll not deny me that, I'm sure!"

So just before cockcrow, Absalon arrived outside the carpenter's house. He had combed and oiled his hair, sewn new ribbons on his coat and was sucking a lozenge to make his breath smell sweet. He tapped gently on the half-open shutter and gave a small cough. "Alison, my pretty love, my little lamb, are you there? Wake up and come to the window! Please come and give me a kiss!"

"Go away, Absalon, you fool!" said Alison scornfully. "I'm not going to kiss you. I love another, a much better man than you. Leave off and let me sleep!"

"True love is always mocked," sighed Absalon. "I know you don't love me, my darling Alison, but please just give me a kiss. Then I promise I will go."

Snug under the covers, Alison giggled to Nicholas lying warm beside her, "I'll give him a kiss he won't forget in a hurry!" And getting out of bed she crossed the room and flung the window wide.

"Come here, Absalon, and kiss me quickly! It's cold in the night air!" Turning her back she bent over and stuck her bare bottom out of the window. Absalon heard her but it was far too dark to see anything at all. He closed his eyes and pursed his lips in blissful expectation – but what was this! Not Alison's lips but her naked bottom! And to make matters worse, at that moment, both Alison and Nicholas burst out laughing. "What a joke!" gasped Nicholas. And the joke was all on Absalon.

As the poor clerk, angry and humiliated, tracked back in the darkness towards town he began to plot his revenge. "That Nicholas!" he fumed. "I'll pay him back for this! I'm not going to let him get away with making a fool of me! And as for Alison, I don't care two pins about her now!"

On his way he passed the door of Gervase the blacksmith, who was already at his forge. "Absalon! What are you doing here at this hour?" But Absalon was in no mood for friendly greetings. "Give me that branding-iron," he said, pointing to an iron heating in the fire and already glowing red-hot. "I'll bring it straight back to you."

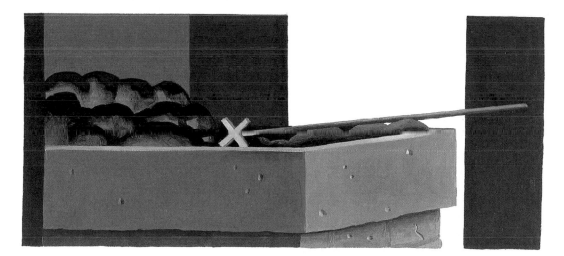

Gervase was surprised at his request but, after a glance at the clerk's set face, he gave him the hot iron without a word.

Back to the carpenter's house went Absalon and stood again outside the window. "Alison, my little flower," he called. "I've brought you a present. Come, let me have a kiss and I'll give it to you!"

"It's Absalon again!" said Nicholas. "This is too much! This time it's my turn to teach him a lesson!" And striding across the room he flung open the window and he too stuck out his bottom.

Absalon was ready with his iron and stuck it fair and square in the middle of the scholar's rump. Nicholas leapt into the air, bellowing with pain. "Help! Hi! Water! Quick! Water! Help!"

Old John the carpenter, sleeping in his barrel, woke up at the cries of "Water!" "The flood has come!" he cried. And taking up his axe he cut the ropes holding the barrel to the ceiling, and down he crashed, barrel and all.

The noise brought Nicholas and Alison tumbling down the stairs shouting, "Help! Murder!" Within minutes the house was full of nosy neighbours crowding round, all standing staring down at poor old John sitting stunned on the floor among the splintered remnants of his barrel.

"He's mad!" said Nicholas. And Alison came chiming in, "It's true – my husband's mad! He's got some nonsense into his head that Noah's flood had come again!" Everyone laughed and talked of the poor carpenter and his suffering as a colossal joke.

And so John was punished for his jealousy; just as Absalon had his comeuppance in kissing Alison's behind; and Nicholas his deserts by being branded on the bottom. And this is how the world wags on.

The Reeve,
or steward, was old, thin and bad-tempered.
His arms and legs were like sticks,
his hair was cropped and beard shaved down
to the stubble. But he knew his job,
and ran his lord's farms with
a firm hand. He himself had a pleasant
house and a good sum of money put by.
His horse, a grey, went by the name of Scot.

THE REEVE

THE REEVE'S TALE

AT TRUMPINGTON near Cambridge there stood a mill. Simpkin the miller was a stout, red-faced man who had grown rich by stealing from the corn brought to him to grind. His wife, the only daughter of the local parson, gave herself tremendous airs and would swagger about town sneering at all the tradespeople, whom she considered beneath her. This charming couple had two children: a baby, only a few months old, and a grown-up daughter. The daughter was fat and plain and few would have noticed her had it not been that her grandfather, the parson, had made her his heir.

One of Simpkin's most valued customers was the bursar of one of the colleges in Cambridge. It was this man's job to bring the college corn to be ground but recently he had fallen ill. Simpkin had been taking advantage of his absence by stealing twice and three times the amount of corn he usually took for himself. The warden of the college complained but the miller didn't care and nothing was done until two penniless students, two friends, decided to take the matter in hand. One was called Alan and the other John, and both came from the same village in the north. With the warden's permission they took a horse, loaded it with corn, and went off to the mill.

"Good day, Simpkin," Alan greeted the miller. "Our bursar's still very ill – like enough to die, I wouldn't wonder – so I have come with my friend John to bring corn for grinding."

"Right you are, lads!" said the miller. "Give me the corn – but what will you do while I grind it?"

"Well," said John, "I think I'll stay here. I've never seen corn grinding and I'd like to watch it right here, going into hopper."

"Aye, so would I," said Alan. "I'll stand over there and watch meal come out into trough. That'd be interesting."

The miller smiled to himself. "The silly fools! They think they can catch me out. But I'll steal twice as much and in front of their very noses! I'll teach them to try to get the better of me!"

As soon as the two students were absorbed in watching their corn, the miller slipped out round the back into the yard where their horse was tethered. Untying its halter he gave it a good slap on the rump which sent it galloping out of the yard and off into the fens. Then he went back inside, saying nothing of what he had done.

When the corn was ground and tied up in a sack, John wandered out and saw their horse was gone. "Lor! Alan, come quick! Warden's horse – it's gone!" Alan rushed out to look, forgetting all about the corn and the miller's thieving tricks.

"Eh, lad, we're in trouble! Quick after it! Coom on!" And off they ran towards the fen, leaving the miller to help himself generously to their flour.

"I'm more than a match for those two clever clogs!" he chuckled to his wife.

Meanwhile Alan and John were splashing about all over the fen whistling and calling to their horse, which showed no desire to bring its moment of liberty to an end, and it was dark before at last they were able to catch him. Exhausted and soaked to the skin they returned to the mill to stable the horse and beg Simpkin to give them a room for the night.

"A room?" said Simpkin grinning broadly at the sight of the two sodden students. "I've no room but what you see here. But if you can pay you're welcome to bed down with us."

"We'll pay," said John eagerly, feeling in his purse. "And Simpkin, give us a bite of food and summat to drink. We need a bit to put inside! Look, here's silver. Here's enough for a meal for both of us and a bed for the night."

So the miller fetched a jug of ale and his wife put a goose on the spit to roast. While it was cooking Simpkin made up a bed for Alan and John, right next to the one which he shared with his wife. Beside it stood the baby's cradle. His daughter had her bed in the same room. There was no other.

The evening passed merrily, with a good dinner, plenty of talk, a crackling fire and several jugs of the miller's strongest ale. Just before midnight Simpkin and his wife, both of them far from sober, went reeling off to bed. Having first made sure the baby was snug in its cradle they fell at once into a drunken sleep, the two of them snoring loud enough to be heard on the outskirts of Cambridge itself. Soon after this Alan and John, too, and the miller's daughter, made their way to bed.

The two men lay there in the dark listening to the noisy and unfragrant chorus coming from the miller's bed. Alan poked John in the ribs. "Did you ever hear such a racket?" he whispered. "We won't get a wink of sleep at this rate! But never mind, I know what I'm going to do. Since that miller, crafty bugger, has tricked us for sure and stolen our flour, I'm going to pay him back in kind. I'll nip into his daughter's bed and count that a fair exchange!"

"Oh, be careful, Alan! Miller's got a wicked temper! If he catches you he'll go mad!"

"Don't give a fig for that!" snorted Alan, and slipping from beneath the covers he crept across the room and into the girl's bed. So deeply was she sleeping that she didn't hear his step nor wake until he was in bed beside her. And then she made not a murmur.

John, meanwhile, lay sleepless in bed envying Alan his daring. "Cor, what a chance to miss! I'll look a right monkey after this! Look at him, with miller's daughter in his arms, and here am I with nothing! Well, the Lord helps those, they say, who help themselves." And up he got and quietly pulled the baby's cradle across the floor until it lay beside his bed. Then he lay down again, to wait.

Soon after this the miller's wife stopped snoring and awoke. She got out of bed and left the room. Returning after a few minutes she fumbled her way in the dark, failed to find the cradle in its usual place by her bed and, believing she had lost her path, groped about until her fingers felt its familiar shape as it lay, now, beside the students' bed. "That was a close thing," she sniggered to herself. "Nearly got in the wrong bed!" And she climbed in beside John.

When the first cock began to crow Alan kissed the miller's daughter goodbye. "Goodbye, my love," said she. "Take care. And, listen, on your way out, as you go past the mill, you'll find behind the main door the bag of meal I helped my father steal from your sack."

They kissed again and Alan got out of bed and started to make his way across the room, so that, when dawn broke, he would be found lying beside John. Suddenly he stubbed his toe against the cradle. "By heck! That were lucky escape! This must be miller's bed." And round he turned to go back to what he took to be John's bed which was, of course, the bed in which Simpkin lay.

Alan slid in under the blanket and, believing the sleeping form next to him to be that of his friend, shook him awake, hissing in his ear, "John! Wake up and listen to this! I've spent the whole night with miller's daughter, while you've been snoring on your back!"

The miller jerked upright. "You scoundrel! You filthy rat!" he bellowed. Seizing Alan by the neck he tried to throttle him but Alan clenched his fist and punched him on the nose. Soon the two of them were down on the floor, fighting like a couple of dogs in a sack. As they staggered about the room the miller fell against John's bed, in which his wife was lying. She woke with a start and began screaming with terror, "Help! Husband, help! The devil is amongst us!" And, jumping out of bed, she grabbed the poker and brought it down, whack! on her husband's head.

With a groan the miller fell back unconscious, while quick as a flash Alan and John, throwing on their clothes, ran out to the yard, untied the horse, picked up their bag of meal – not forgetting the stolen portion behind the door – and back to Cambridge they went.

So Simpkin the miller was paid in his own coin – done out of money for the dinner, done out of money for grinding the corn and tricked over his wife and daughter.

Do as you would be done by – as the motto goes!

❧

*T*hree Priests

were travelling with the Nun, and one of them,

mounted on a thin, ugly little horse,

was a most amiable fellow,

always ready to please and to

entertain the others.

THE NUN'S PRIEST

THE NUN'S PRIEST'S TALE

THERE WAS ONCE an old widow who lived in a tiny cottage on the edge of a meadow, just outside the village and near to a little wood. Here she housed three pigs, three cows and a sheep known as Molly. The widow was poor but she lived simply and by working hard had always managed to feed herself and her two daughters. Their meals, it is true, were plain – milk, brown bread, boiled bacon and eggs – but they all three enjoyed good spirits and the best of health. At the back of the cottage was a farmyard surrounded by a high picket-fence and here the widow kept seven hens and a cock called Chanticleer.

Chanticleer was a handsome bird and when it came to crowing he had no rival. His "cock-a-doodle-doo!" louder than the church bells on Sunday, was famous for its pitch and clarity. His comb, battlemented like a castle wall, was a deep coral red, his beak was jet black, his legs were a brilliant blue, while his glossy plumage shone like jewelled enamel. The seven hens Chanticleer kept under his wing – he was their lord and master. The loveliest, she with the softest feathers and the darkest eye, was known as Lady Pertelote and she was Chanticleer's favourite wife. From the day she first broke out of the egg she had loved Chanticleer with all her heart. They were a devoted pair and it was a joy to hear them sing together every dawn.

One morning before first light, when Chanticleer and all his hens were still roosting in the rafters of the widow's roof, the cock suddenly began to groan and tremble in his sleep. Pertelote, perched beside him, woke with a start. "Dearest heart," she said, "what is the matter? What a noise you're making – you gave me quite a fright!"

"Oh," groaned Chanticleer, "I've had such a terrible nightmare! My heart is still racing! I dreamt I was in the yard outside when a fearful beast came creeping up behind me. It was like a large dog, russet coloured, with ears tipped with black, and golden glowing eyes. A dreadful monster, enough to make me die of fright!"

"Shame on you!" cried Pertelote. "What a coward you are, to be so frightened by a dream! Bad dreams are nothing but the symptom of indigestion. You must have eaten something that's disagreed with you, that's all. You must take a purge. I'll make it up for you myself – herbs from the farmyard, a little ground-ivy and hellebore, and perhaps a couple of worms to clear the system. That will put you right. And let's hear no more of bad dreams."

"Well, madam, you may be right. But you have only to look at the past to see that dreams can carry great significance. Why, only recently I read that story of the two friends who, arriving in a strange town late at night, were forced to lodge in separate houses as the town was full. In the middle of the night one dreamed that the other was calling to him, calling for help, crying out that he was being murdered. He awoke in terror but, knowing it to be a dream, dismissed it from his mind, turned over and went back to sleep.

The dream returned; again he put it from him. The third time he fell asleep he dreamt his friend came to him, a bleeding corpse, crying, 'Too late! I have been slain! Dear comrade, you must avenge my death! In the morning, go to the town's west gate and there you will see a cart loaded with dung. In that cart will you find my body.'

"And, madam," continued Chanticleer, "it turned out true, just as in the dream. His friend did as he'd been told – the west gate, the dung cart – and demanded that the authorities be fetched. The cart was overturned and there indeed was the body of the murdered man. The carter was arrested, tried, found guilty and hanged. And so justice was done, all as the result of a dream! So you see, dear wife, one must take these things seriously.

"But now, enough of dreams!" Chanticleer stood up and flapped his gorgeous wings. "I have only to look on the beautiful scarlet of your face for all my cares to disappear!"

With these loving words he flew down from his perch, calling his little troupe out into the early light. Once more ruler of the roost he clucked and strutted and pecked upon the ground. Full of himself and of the joy of life and the freshness of the May morning he threw back his head and crowed loudly with happiness – unaware that at that very moment Fate was preparing her blow.

The night before a fox, with black-tipped ears and bushy tail, had broken through the stockade and into the farmyard. All night he had lain in the cabbage patch near to where Chanticleer and his wives were accustomed to feed. There he crouched, still as a stone, watching his prey.

Pertelote and her sisters were enjoying a leisurely dust-bath; Chanticleer was singing merrily to himself, merry as a mermaid (and we all know how merrily mermaids sing). His eye was on a butterfly about to light on a cabbage-leaf. Suddenly he saw the fox. He gave a fearful start, knowing at once that he was looking in the face of his enemy. "Cock, cock," he stammered, and would have fled, but the fox began to speak.

"Why do you start, Sir Chanticleer? Don't be afraid. I am a friend; indeed one of your greatest admirers. It is widely known that you are possessed of a magnificent voice and I came here purely for the pleasure of hearing you sing. And may I say that, before I heard you, there was no singer I rated more highly than your late, much respected father. How musical he was! What wonderful technique! The way he used to stand on tiptoe with his neck stretched out, each note issuing perfect from his slender beak! Oh, Sir, I beg you, let me hear your voice! Let me hear you out-sing your father!"

Hearing these honeyed words and fatally innocent of the fox's treacherous intent, Chanticleer raised himself up on his claws, stretched up his neck, closed his eyes and began full-throatedly to sing. The fox leapt. Grabbing the bird by the neck he flung him over his shoulder and galloped off towards the wood.

Fortunately Pertelote saw what was happening, and she and her sisters set up a cackle loud enough to raise the dead. The widow, hearing the clamour, glanced out of the window to see the fox streaking towards the wood with Chanticleer flat along his back.

"Look! Look!" she cried to her two daughters. "A fox has got our cock!" And, each taking up a stick, they ran after him. And across the meadow in their wake ran the farmhands, yelling and cursing, and the village boys, and after them the dogs Coll, Rover, Spot and Jack;

then the cows and the calf; and the pigs, frightened by the barking dogs; and last of all Molly the sheep.

The men and women cursed and shouted as they tore after the fox. The ducks quacked and flapped in fright out of the pond; the geese in terror flew up onto the roof-tops; even the bees, alarmed, swarmed out of their hive, as the hue and cry, stumbling and yelling, blowing on whistles and beating on sticks, streamed across the fields on the fleeing fox's trail.

In desperate peril though he was, Chanticleer at last came to his senses. "Sir fox," he managed to croak from his uncomfortable position across the fox's back, "why do you let yourself be pursued by these bumpkins? Tell them to turn back! Now that we have reached the wood, make them leave you to enjoy your prey in peace!"

"Why, yes, he's right," thought the fox, and opened his mouth to reply. At which moment the nimble cock flapped his wings and flew high into the trees. The fox, too late, saw his mistake. "Dear Chanticleer," he oozed, his wicked yellow eyes staring up through the new green leaves, "I didn't mean to hurt you. Please come down and I'll tell you exactly what I meant. No harm, I promise you."

"Come down? No, not I," said Chanticleer, safe on his branch. "I'm not such a fool as to be tricked twice. Your flattery won't work on me a second time. From now on my eyes will stay open!"

He threw back his head and crowed a triumphant song to his salvation – and to the power of dreams!

❧

*T*he Pardoner

was a smooth-faced man with yellow greasy locks,

the bulging eyes of a hare and a

silly little voice like a goat's.

He made a fat living selling pardons to the

guilty, and in church knew

very well how to part the congregation

from its money.

THE PARDONER

THE PARDONER'S TALE

THREE YOUNG hooligans were sitting playing cards in a tavern, already more than half drunk, although it was still only the middle of the morning. As they cursed and quarrelled over their game, they suddenly heard a ringing outside – the small, clear sound of the handbell that accompanies a coffin on its journey to the churchyard. The three men looked up from their play and the eldest called out to the pot-boy, "Boy, go and find out who is being buried, whose corpse is in the coffin! Hurry up! Look sharp about it!"

"Sir, no need to find out. I know who it is. He used to be a friend of yours, Sir. He was killed last night. He'd passed out, Sir, from the drink, and was lying there on that bench. A local fellow, known round here as Death, came creeping up on him and knifed him through the heart. And then the fellow vanished, just like that, without a word. Death, he's killed a thousand, I should say, during this present epidemic of the plague. If you come across him, Sir, it would pay you to treat him with respect. Be on your guard – that's what my mother always tells me."

"Too true," the publican came chiming in. "This year alone, for instance, he's killed every man, woman and child in that big village down the road. He must live round there, I think. So watch how you go, and be prepared!"

But this warning served only to excite the three ruffians to anger. The eldest banged his fist on the table. "The hell with him!" he swore, his face purple with rage and drink. "Who does he think he is! We're not scared. He doesn't frighten me, I tell you. We'll search him out, street by street, until we find him. But first let's make a

vow: a pact of brotherhood – each to defend the other. And we'll kill this fellow Death before tonight!"

The three of them lurched upright and clasping their hands together, swore their oath. Then they staggered out, boastful and defiant. "If we can only catch him, Death is as good as dead!" they shouted as they started off in the direction of the village which the publican had described.

Hardly had they gone half a mile, when they passed on the road an old man, thin and poorly dressed. He greeted them politely. But the leader of the brawling trio rudely pushed past. "Get out of our way, you old fool! What are you doing alive? At your age, you should be dead!"

"I am still alive," replied the man, looking the young brute steadily in the eye, "because, search as I will, I can find no one prepared to exchange his youth for my old age. Not even Death himself will take my life. And so I must continue to walk the earth, ill and tired though I am.

"But you, Sir, why do you speak so roughly to me? Have you never been taught to show respect to your elders? You would be wise to do to others as you would be done by. And now, please let me pass: I must be on my way."

"Not so fast!" brayed the braggart, seizing the old man by the arm. "You spoke of Death. Obviously you know him – so tell us where to find him. Or it'll be the worse for you!"

The old man smiled, and disengaged his arm. "Well, Sirs, there I can help you. If it's Death you want –" and here his eyes sparkled as though at some private joke – "just go up there, up that path you see on your left, and on towards the wood. I saw him there earlier today, sitting waiting under the big oak. You can't miss him! God bless you, and good day!"

Without waiting to give thanks for these directions, the three bullies broke into a run, and soon reached the little wood. There indeed was the big oak, and under it they saw, to their astonishment, lying on the ground a great golden gleaming pile of newly minted coins.

Instantly all thoughts of Death went from their minds, so greedy were they for the gold.

The ringleader spoke first. "Brothers, listen. It's quite clear that we were meant to find this gold. It belongs to us. Easy come, easy go. We'll spend it exactly as we please, and there's enough here for us to live in luxury for the rest of our days.

"But how to get it away? If we're seen with it, people will think we're robbers, and we'll risk a hanging. No, much better to wait till dark and then we'll carry it back to town. Are you all agreed?"

The others nodded eagerly.

"Now, let's draw lots: the one who picks the shortest straw shall run back to the inn to fetch wine and something to eat, while the other two stay here on guard. Then as soon as night falls, the three of us will carry the gold back and hide it in one of our houses."

He picked up three straws and held them out. The youngest drew the shortest straw, and off he ran at once to town.

As soon as he was out of sight, his two companions sat down and the leader, the wickedest of the three, began to speak. "You know, don't you, that you can trust me like a brother?"

"We're sworn to that."

"Good. Now listen carefully. Here's all this gold to be divided between the three of us. Would you not take it kindly, if I could work out a way for you and me to have half each?"

"Well, yes. But how? He —" he gestured with his head towards the town — "he knows the gold is one third his. What are we to tell him when he comes back?"

"Don't you worry about that. Do I have your word that we two act together? If so, I'll tell you how it shall be done."

"You have my word."

"Right. Now, there are two of us against his one. When he gets back here, you get up and, as though in fun, pretend to have a friendly wrestle with him. Then, once you get him on the ground, I'll stab him in the back. Then, while you and he are struggling, you do the same, and stick your dagger through his heart. That should do the trick. And all this money will be ours, just yours and mine. Imagine that!"

Meanwhile the youngest, running towards the town, began to think of that great shining pile of treasure, and to wish that it could be his alone. At this moment, the Devil, never one to let slip an opportunity, put it into the young thug's head that he could poison both his friends, and thus be sole possessor of the gold.

As soon as he reached town, the youth ran straight to an apothecary for some strong poison. "I've got some rats I want to get rid of," he explained. "And a polecat that's been after my hens."

"I've got just the thing," said the chemist reaching down a box of powder from a high shelf. "This stuff here's so strong that if any living creature so much as touch it with his tongue, he'll drop down dead. Right on the spot. It's that strong, you see."

The black-hearted young man bought the box of powder and went with it to a nearby house where he found a man who gave him three bottles. Into two of them, he poured the poison – careful to leave one clean for his own consumption – then filled all three to the top with wine.

Back he went to his two companions waiting underneath the tree. Everything happened smoothly, exactly as was planned. The two ruffians fell on the third, stabbing him to death. As he lay lifeless on the ground, the elder of the two said, "Come on: let's sit down and have a drink to celebrate. We've got the rest of our lives to spend the money. And in a minute we'll have to get up our strength to bury that corpse there." They sat down, and each picked up a bottle. They drew out the corks with their teeth. They drank the poisoned wine. And so they died.

Thus Death came, as he always does, sooner or later.

~

*T*he Wife of Bath

was a woman of experience: she had travelled

three times to Jerusalem,

had had five husbands, and there was

little she didn't know about the workings of

the world. Now red-faced and stout,

she was still handsome, and took pleasure in

wearing scarlet stockings and

big, startling hats.

THE WIFE OF BATH

THE WIFE OF BATH'S TALE

LONG AGO, back in King Arthur's time, there lived a Knight known for his love of pleasure. Riding by the river one day, he met a pretty girl walking by herself and, ignoring all her pleas, he threw her to the ground and attacked her. King Arthur, when he heard of it, was outraged, and condemned the man to death. But Guinevere and her ladies, appalled that so young a knight should die, implored the King to spare him. The Queen herself begged so earnestly that Arthur at length relented. He said that the case was now in her hands, and that she could do as she liked, show the man mercy, or not, as she chose.

Guinevere summoned the Knight to come before her. "You are," she sternly told him, "in danger of losing your head. But I will give you one chance to save yourself. You shall go free if you can, within a year, bring me the answer to this question: what is it that women most desire?"

The Knight bowed humbly and promised to return in twelve months with the answer – or forfeit his life. With a sinking heart, he rode away from the castle.

As the weeks passed, he travelled to the furthest corners of the kingdom. But wherever he went, at every door at which he knocked, country or town, he was given a different answer to his question. Some said that what women wanted was riches; others, fun and a good time; some said honour; clothes, said some, or flattery, or a handsome husband.

A year passed and still the Knight had not found the answer. His time was up, he knew it, and his life must soon be at an end. On the

last day of the twelfth month, he was mournfully riding homewards when, in a grassy clearing on the edge of a wood, he caught sight of a company of ladies dancing. Eagerly he spurred towards them in the hope that they perhaps would tell him what he had to know, but before he reached them, they vanished into air. He saw only one old woman, a hideous old hag sitting squat upon the ground.

"Sir Knight," she called to him. "What are you seeking? Tell me, for I may be able to help you."

"Madam, I wish you could. Unless I can discover what it is that women most desire, I am as good as dead. If you can tell me that, I'll pay whatever price you name."

The crone fixed him with a bleary eye. "Swear to do what I ask," she croaked, "and I'll tell you the answer to your question."

"I swear," the Knight replied.

The old woman, pulling him down towards her, whispered a few words in his ear. "Now your life is safe," she said. "You have nothing more to fear."

With a light heart and his life restored, the Knight, obeying her demand, helped the old woman up into his saddle, and together they made the journey to King Arthur's court. There, in the great hall, the Knight stood before the Queen, who was surrounded by her ladies of every age and status – matrons, widows and young girls. A hush fell on the company as the Knight prepared to speak.

"Madam," he said, "I have the answer to your question: what every woman wants is to rule her man. That is her greatest wish. Now kill me, or spare me. I await your decision."

At these words, the ladies clapped their hands and the Queen rose to her feet. "Sir, you have spoken the truth – and in so doing you have won your life."

The ladies nodded and smiled approvingly. Only the old hag remained unsmiling. Her expression grim, she stepped forward to address the Queen.

"My lady, I beg you to see justice done! It was I who told this Knight the answer to your question, and in return he promised to give me whatever I asked. And what I ask is this: that you, Sir Knight, should take me for your wife."

"Oh, come now, madam! I know that is what I said, but for God's sake choose something else – my house, my lands, but not, please not, my person!"

"I may be old and I may be ugly, but there's nothing else I want. I want to be your wife and your heart's love."

The Knight cursed out loud that such a cruel fate should be his, but there was no escape: his word had been given. He and the old hag were married the very next day. The ceremony itself was brief, and it was followed by no festivities. The wretched bridegroom skulked in a corner most of the day, dreading the moment when he would have to take his hideous wife to bed.

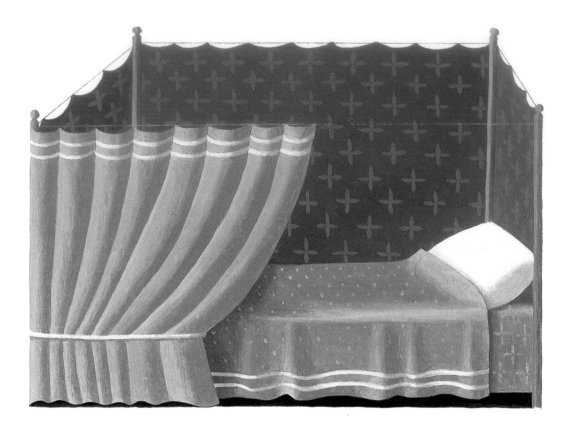

When night fell, he accompanied her to the bridal chamber, then threw himself on the marriage bed and turned his face to the wall.

His wife lay down beside him, and smilingly she asked him, "Is this the way a husband should treat his wife on their wedding day? What have I done to deserve this unchivalrous behaviour? Tell me, so that I may put it right."

"Put it right!" the Knight exclaimed. "No, that's impossible! My life is ruined! Here I am, shackled for ever to a wife who is ill-bred, poor and monstrously ugly. How can that be put right!"

"Is that what's troubling you? Now, husband, listen to me. You say I am ill-bred: but virtue comes from the heart, not from ancient lineage or great possessions. The humblest beggar can be more truly a gentleman than the greatest nobleman in the kingdom. As for being poor, there is no shame in that: those without possessions are often richer in happiness than the miser tormented by envy of his neighbour's wealth. That I am old and ugly, I do not deny: but old age is worthy of respect; and surely you would prefer to have an ugly wife, who is never likely to be seduced by another man, than to be the jealous husband of a faithless beauty?

"I will now give you the choice: would you rather have me old and ugly, but constant and obedient to your every whim? Or young and pretty, and flirting with all the good-looking men who come to the house? The choice is yours."

The Knight was silent for several minutes. Then he groaned and rubbed his eyes. "My dear wife, it is for you to decide. I put the whole matter into your hands. Whatever pleases you is right."

"I am to have my own way?"

"Certainly."

"Then all is well! Come, kiss me, and I will give you everything! You shall have me young and beautiful, and as faithful as ever wife was to her husband since the beginning of the world! Now open the curtains, my dearest husband, and look at me."

The Knight drew back the curtains and looked at her, and there she was as fresh and young and lovely as a spring morning. He caught her in his arms and covered her with kisses. And so began a long and happy marriage that lasted in perfect amity and bliss to their lives' end.

The Franklin
was a well-to-do landowner who loved the good
things of life. He kept an excellent table,
and was known throughout the
country as a generous host whose house was
always open and welcome to both
friends and neighbours.

THE FRANKLIN

THE FRANKLIN'S TALE

IN BRITTANY there lived a knight who had courted his lady so long and ardently that she at last granted him her hand in marriage. As a pledge of his love, he promised on their wedding day that he would never insist that she obey him, nor would he ever give in to jealousy. She, for her part, thanked him for his generosity and swore that she would always be a true and faithful wife. And so they lived in perfect happiness for nearly a year.

Then the time came for Arveragus, for so the knight was called, to leave for the wars overseas. At his departure, Dorigen, his wife, was inconsolable: every night she cried herself to sleep and spent all day longing only for his return. But as the weeks passed, she gradually grew calmer and allowed herself to be coaxed by her friends into enjoying life a little, and occasionally turning her mind to subjects other than her husband's absence.

But one anxiety never ceased to haunt her. The castle in which she lived was on the sea, overlooking the water's edge. Almost daily Dorigen walked on the ramparts and as she gazed down at the water, at the cruel black rocks that ringed the shore, she would sigh, "Alas, I would to God these horrid, jagged rocks would sink to Hell. What if my husband should be wrecked and drowned as so many poor wretches have been drowned on this very spot before!"

Her friends, seeing how it grieved Dorigen to be in sight of the sea, encouraged her to walk inland, in the woods and fields. One morning in early summer they took her to a nearby garden where a picnic had been laid. It was the softest, freshest time of year, and after they had eaten, the whole company danced on the grass, singing gaily as they danced — all except for Dorigen who sat miserably apart, pining for her husband.

Among the men dancing on the lawn was a young squire, Aurelius, who for more than two years had been secretly in love with Dorigen. He had never dared speak to her of his love, but when she was near would sigh meaningfully as though suffering from some deep private sorrow. Now, with Arveragus away, Aurelius thought he saw his chance. Kneeling beside Dorigen he said, "Madam, I know that this is a time of sadness for you, but I must implore you to take pity on me. I have loved you so long and suffered so much."

"What are you saying?" Dorigen exclaimed. "I can hardly believe it! Surely you know that I shall never be unfaithful to my husband?" Then she laughed at the stricken expression on the young man's face and added teasingly, "But I tell you what, Aurelius: I'll make a bargain with you. Take those hateful rocks from round the coast and I promise you I will be yours!"

Aurelius gasped. "But, madam, that's impossible! Is there no other way to win you?"

"No, no other way," said Dorigen, and dismissing the subject from her mind, rose to her feet and walked quickly off to join her friends who were preparing to return home.

Aurelius, however, sat as though turned to stone. "All hope is gone," he said to himself. "There is nothing left for me to do but die of unrequited love."

Time passed. Arveragus returned home from the wars, in the best of health and covered in glory. Dorigen was happier than words can describe. Husband and wife were now never apart, spending all of each day blissfully together.

Two years went by, and still the young squire languished in misery, sick and thin for love of Dorigen. Although he had told no one but her of his love, at last he decided to confide in his brother, whom he had always trusted.

His brother, who had long feared for Aurelius's life, was glad to learn the cause of his despair. He remembered that, as a student in

Orleans, he had read a little on the subject of astrology; and it now occurred to him that an astrologer might be the very person to help his brother. He went to Aurelius and told him this, and encouraged him with such spirit that the young man got up off his bed and agreed to go immediately to Orleans.

Without any delay, the two brothers set off. Coming within sight of the city, they met a friendly young scholar who fell into conversation with them. After a few minutes of polite exchange, he surprised them by telling them that he knew the purpose of their journey, and that he could help them. He then invited them to come to his house that evening.

The magician, for so he was, gave them an excellent dinner, and after they had eaten, he conjured up a series of magic scenes: they saw, as clearly as if it were happening in the room in which they sat, a pack of hounds in pursuit of a stag; then a hawk flying at a heron. The scene changed to knights jousting at a tournament; then Aurelius was entranced to see Dorigen dancing, and he in the scene dancing with her. Suddenly the magician clapped his hands and the pictures vanished.

Aurelius, excited and impressed by this display of the magician's art, begged him to try to remove the rocks from the coast of Brittany. And what would be his price? The man at first was reluctant to commit himself, then demanded the enormous sum of a thousand pounds. "A thousand pounds!" Aurelius cried. "You shall have it! It's a bargain! I'd give you the world if it belonged to me, if only you can do as you say!"

The next day the brothers, accompanied by the magician, returned to Brittany. The magician, pitying the state Aurelius was in, studied hard to work out how he could achieve the illusion that the rocks along the coast had been spirited away. And so, cleverly taking into account the time of year, the state of the tides and the position of the moon and stars, he calculated how to make it seem as though the waters had risen and washed the rocks away by magic. And indeed for a week or more it looked as though the rocks had disappeared.

Aurelius was in raptures. Falling to his knees, he thanked the magician with all his heart; then hurried to where he knew he would find his lady, Dorigen. "Madam," he said, bowing low before her. "I have done as you commanded. I do not ask anything of you, but to remember what you promised." And with that he left her.

Dorigen hurried to the sea-shore, and as she gazed out over the water the colour drained from her face. "How could such a thing, such a monstrous miracle have occurred! What shall I do?" And she crept home, cold with fear. Arveragus was away for a few days, and Dorigen flung herself down on her bed to cry and bewail her fate. "What trap have I fallen into? I must either kill myself or betray my marriage vows!" She went over and over the problem in her mind, tormenting herself with impossible solutions, but deciding nothing.

After three days Arveragus returned. Of course he asked at once why she was crying, and Dorigen told him the whole story. "Well, well," said he. "It's perfectly plain that you must keep your word, and I must bear it as best I can. The only thing I ask is that you tell not a living soul of this. Now, wash your face, and let us both look cheerful so no one may guess our trouble."

Dorigen set off for the garden where she had pledged her word to Aurelius. Half-way there she saw him walking towards her. The young man greeted her and asked her where she was going. "To the garden, as my husband told me, oh alas, to keep my promise to you, wretched woman that I am!"

At these words Aurelius felt a great surge of pity both for Dorigen and for the noble knight Arveragus. He saw instantly that it was better he should forgo his passion than that such an honourable lady should be dishonoured. "Madam," he said, "I cannot bear to see you in distress. From this moment I release you from your promise. And for my part I give you my word that I shall never speak of it more. And so you see a squire can behave as nobly as a knight!"

Dorigen fell on her knees with gratitude and thanked him over and over again. Then she went happily home to tell her husband what had taken place.

But now Aurelius was faced with having to pay his debt to the magician. There was no way he could raise the sum other than by selling all he owned. "Perhaps," he thought, "he would allow me a year or two to raise a thousand pounds. Otherwise I shall be ruined." Dejectedly he sought out the man and explained his situation.

"Did I not keep my side of the agreement?" the magician asked.

"Indeed you did," replied Aurelius in a low voice.

"And did you not take possession of the lady?"

"No, no," he faltered. Then at the magician's request told him what had happened.

When he had heard the whole story, the magician clapped him on the shoulder. "My dear sir, each of you behaved as nobly as the other, and men of learning can behave nobly, too. I release you from your debt. I shall take not a penny! And now farewell!" And up he jumped upon his horse and rode back home to Orleans.

❧

INDEX

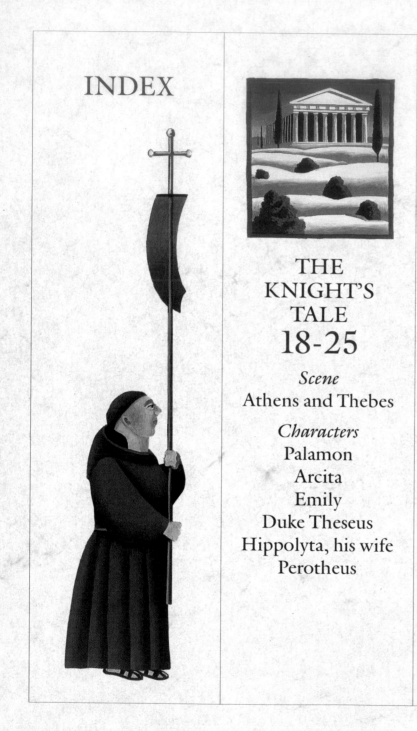

THE NUN'S PRIEST'S TALE
46-51

Scene
n English farmyard

Characters
Chanticleer, a cock
Pertelote, a hen
The fox
A widow

THE PARDONER'S TALE
54-59

Scene
A tavern

Characters
Three hooligans
A publican
An apothecary
Death

THE WIFE OF BATH'S TALE
62-67

Scene
King Arthur's England

Characters
King Arthur
Queen Guinevere
The Knight
An old crone

THE FRANKLIN'S TALE
70-75

Scene
Brittany

Characters
Arveragus
Dorigen, his wife
Aurelius
Aurelius' brother
A magician

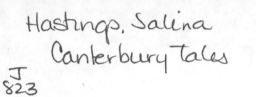